Twelve Days of Christmas Presents

Paintings by Emily Bolam

Sterling Publishing Co., Inc.
New York

Library of Congress Cataloging-in-Publication Data Available.

2 4 6 8 10 9 7 5 3 1

Published by Sterling Publishing Co., Inc.
387 Park Avenue South, New York, NY 10016

Distributed in Canada by Sterling Publishing
c/o Canadian Manda Group, One Atlantic Avenue, Suite 105
Toronto, Ontario, Canada M6K 3E7
Distributed in Great Britain and Europe by Chris Lloyd at Orca Book
Services, Stanley House, Fleets Lane, Poole BH15 3AJ, England
Distributed in Australia by Capricorn Link (Australia) Pty. Ltd.
P.O. Box 704, Windsor, NSW 2756, Australia

Printed in China

Sterling ISBN 1-4027-1700-8

For Santa's helpers everywhere

On the first day of Christmas
my mommy gave to me
a puppy under the tree.

On the second day of Christmas
my daddy gave to me
two storybooks...

and a

under
the
tree.

BOOKSTORE

OPEN

On the third day of Christmas
my grandma gave to me
three hula hoops...

two storybooks

and a

under
the
tree.

On the fourth day of Christmas
my grandpa gave to me
four furry bears...

three hula hoops
two storybooks
and a

under
the
tree.

On the fifth day of Christmas
my sister gave to me
five wind-up toys...

four furry bears
three hula hoops
two storybooks

and a

under
the
tree.

On the sixth day of Christmas
my brother gave to me
six trains a-tooting...

five wind-up toys
four furry bears
three hula hoops
two storybooks
and a

under
the
tree.

On the seventh day of Christmas
my cousins gave to me
seven pots for painting...

six trains a-tooting
five wind-up toys
four furry bears
three hula hoops
two storybooks
and a

under
the
tree.

On the eighth day of Christmas
my auntie gave to me
eight fish a-swimming...

seven pots for painting
six trains a-tooting
five wind-up toys
four furry bears
three hula hoops
two storybooks
and a

under
the
tree.

On the ninth day of Christmas
my uncle gave to me
nine balls a-bouncing...

eight fish a-swimming
seven pots for painting
six trains a-tooting
five wind-up toys
four furry bears
three hula hoops
two storybooks
and a

under
the
tree.

49

On the tenth day of Christmas
my neighbors gave to me
ten jelly babies...

nine balls a-bouncing
eight fish a-swimming
seven pots for painting
six trains a-tooting
five wind-up toys
four furry bears
three hula hoops
two storybooks
and a

under
the
tree.

On the eleventh day of Christmas
my good friends gave to me
eleven cats a-jumping...

ten jelly babies
nine balls a-bouncing
eight fish a-swimming
seven pots for painting
six trains a-tooting
five wind-up toys
four furry bears
three hula hoops
two storybooks
and a

under
the
tree.

On the twelfth day of Christmas
I gave to all my friends
twelve balloons a-flying...

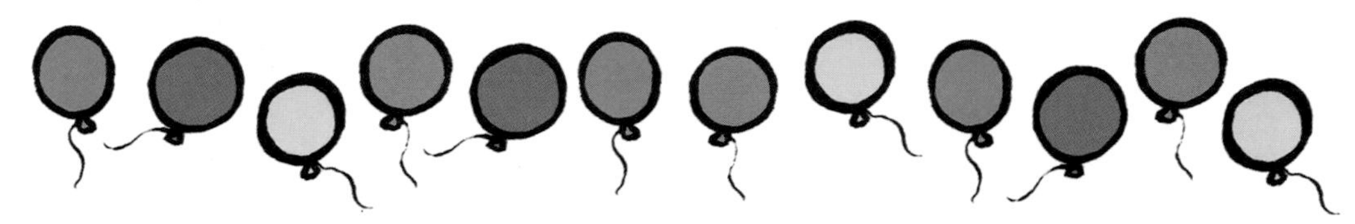

eleven cats a-jumping
ten jelly babies
nine balls a-bouncing
eight fish a-swimming
seven pots for painting
six trains a-tooting
five wind-up toys
four furry bears
three hula hoops
two storybooks
and a

under
the
tree.

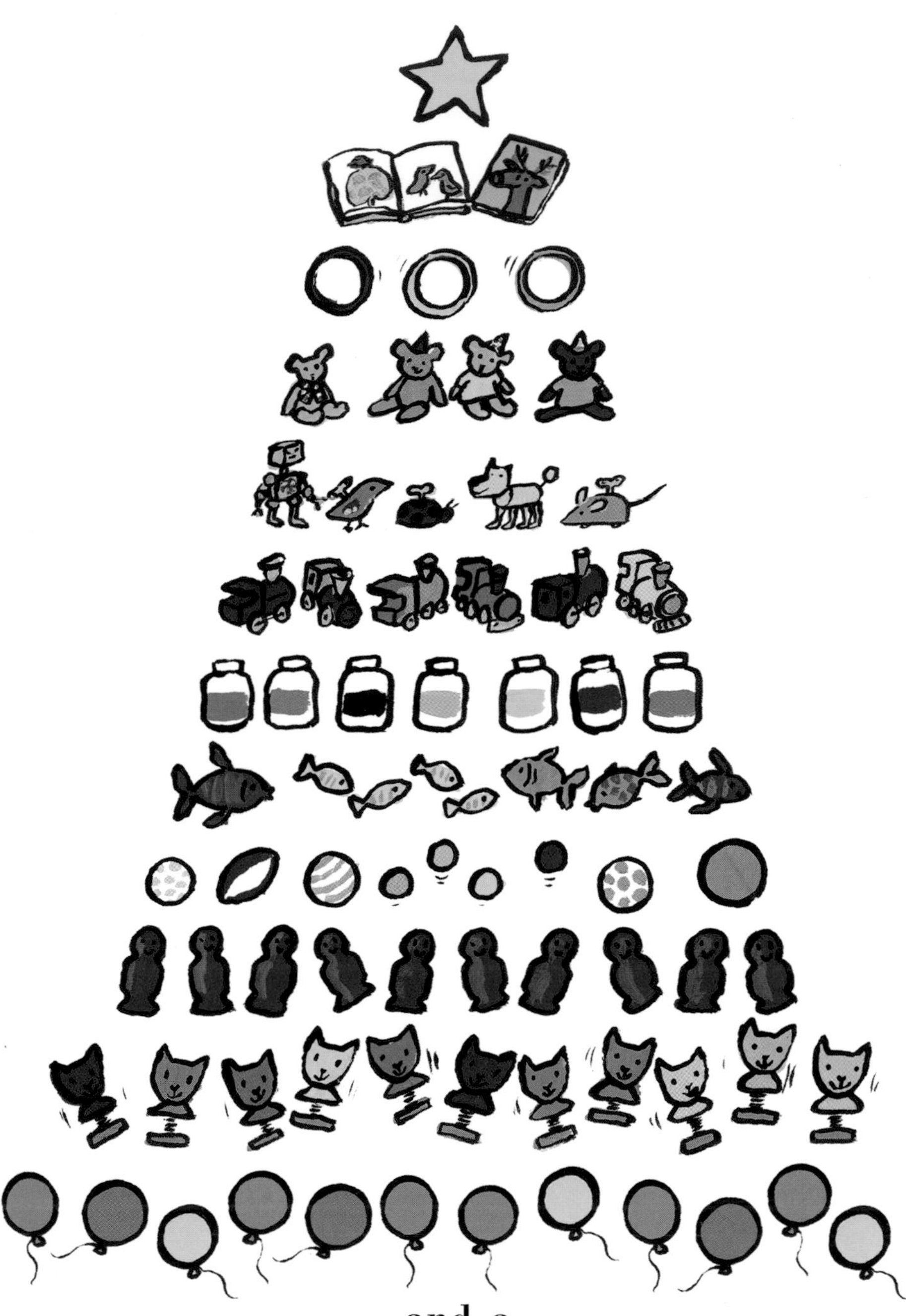

and a

under
the
tree.

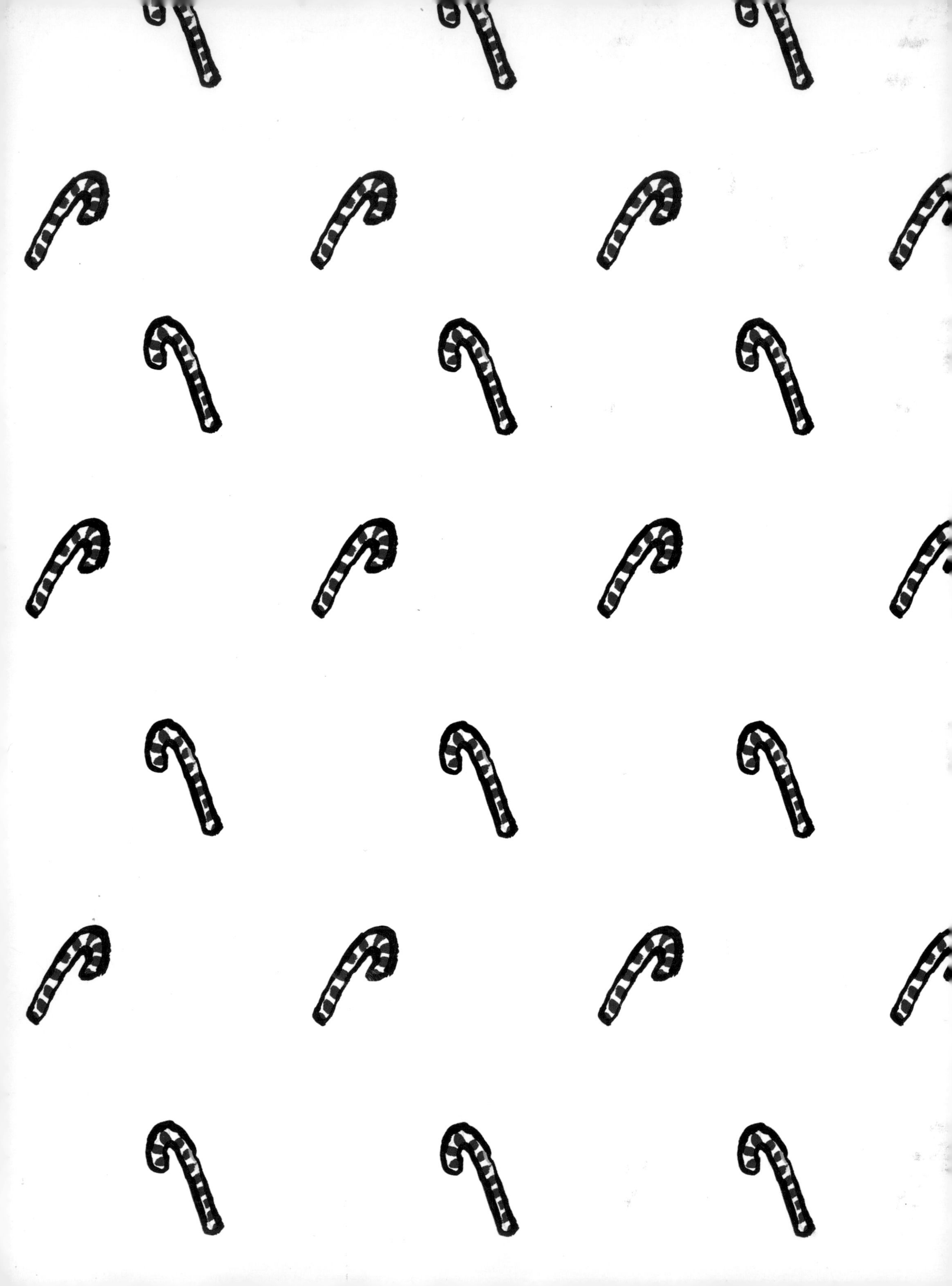